George the Alligator
Finds a Home

Margaret "Ms. Sam" Sansom

Illustrated by Cydney Bittner

George the Alligator

Copyright © 2022 Margaret "Ms. Sam" Sansom

All rights reserved.

Published by Red Penguin Books

Bellerose Village, New York

Library of Congress Control Number: 2022908200

ISBN

Print 978-1-63777-267-6 / 978-1-63777-288-1

Digital 978-1-63777-266-9

No part of this book may be reproduced in any form or by any electronic or mechanical means, including information storage and retrieval systems, without written permission from the author, except for the use of brief quotations in a book review.

"Hey Mom – Michael and Daddy are home!" said Sarah, looking out the window.

Soon the car pulls up to the side of the house.

Michael rushed in the back door.
"Mom. Sarah.
Come see the surprise
Dad and I brought!"

"What is it?" Mom asked.
"It's a new pet we found
at the Rescue Center ."

Mom looked around at the two cats, dog, parrot and hamster.
"Why do we need another pet?"
"But this pet is special," said Michael.

"What happens when he gets bigger?" Mom asked.
Sarah's eyes widened.
"Won't he eat our other pets?"

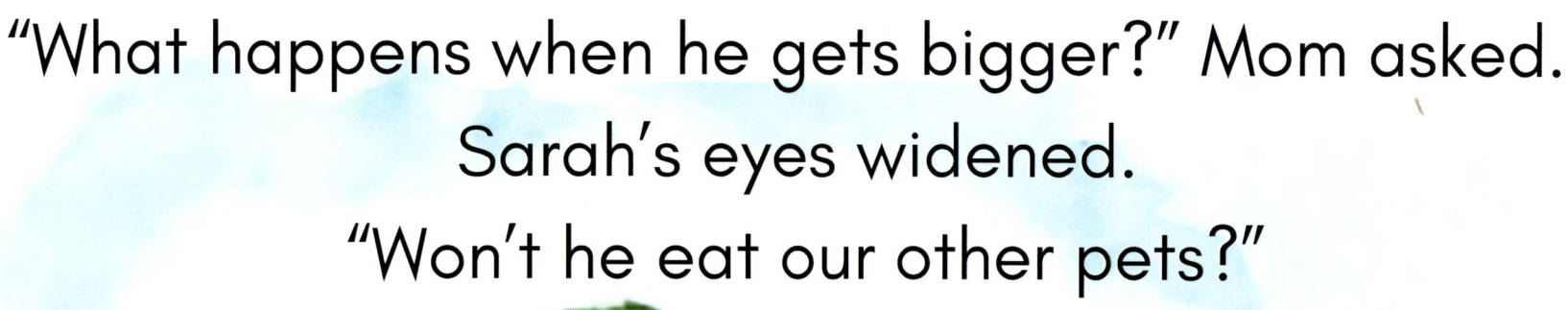

"He is already five years old and he is as big as he'll ever be. Nobody knows why he is so small," Dad replied.

Michael shook his head. "He doesn't have any teeth."

"Where's his tail?" Sarah asked.

"He didn't have a tail or teeth when he hatched," Michael answered. "And he couldn't live in a swamp without a tail to help him swim and turn over."

The alligator moved, and Sarah moved back. Michael said, "He won't hurt you."

Mom frowned, "I just don't think we can keep an alligator as a pet."

"Oh, Mom. He is so gentle, and he'll be the neatest pet ever. We'll be the only people to have an alligator of our very own."

"Well, I don't trust him; he might hurt our other pets," Mother replied, "so we'll have to keep him separated from the rest of them."

"Can we call him George?" Sarah asked.

Then the family decided that George would live in their large backyard.
Michael and Father built a tall chain fence around part of the yard away from the play area.

They dug a big hole in the ground and put a large wading pool into the hole.

Michael's jobs were to feed George and to fill the pool every day because George loved to splash around in the freshwater.

He nodded his head up and down and stomped his feet so hard that there was always a puddle around the pool.

In the first few days, Mom stood right outside the gate and watched closely while Michael was inside the pen.

At first, Sarah would not go inside George's pen. Instead, she stood by the gate while Michael filled the pool, scratched George under his chin, and fed him.

One day, Sarah surprised her parents by asking if she could feed George. They agreed so Sarah filled a huge round pan with vegetables.

George liked fresh fruits and vegetables, but what he enjoyed the most was when Sarah brought him a big slice of pie piled high with ice cream.

For the first month, all the animals spent hours a few feet away from the fence from George's pen watching him.

Whenever George came near the fence, they all quickly scampered away.

One day, while George was asleep,
Squawky the parrot
climbed to the top of the fence
and down the other side.

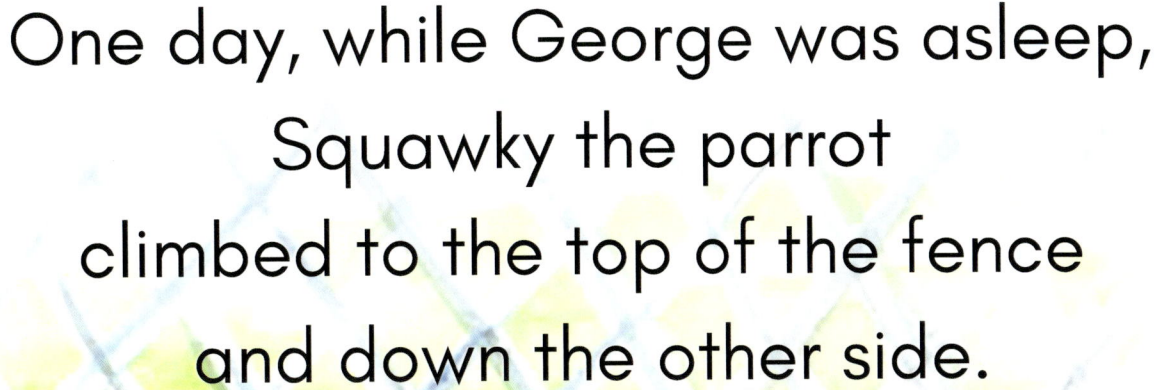

The parrot waddled over close to George and watched until the alligator opened one eye.

Squawky ran as fast as he could back to the fence and scooted back outside the pen.

George just opened his mouth wide, yawned, and went back to sleep.

Day by day, the pets went closer and closer to the fence until one day all of them were right on top of the fence while George was stretched out along the inside.

Eventually, the family took George for rides in the family car.
At first, he sat in the back seat right behind Mom.

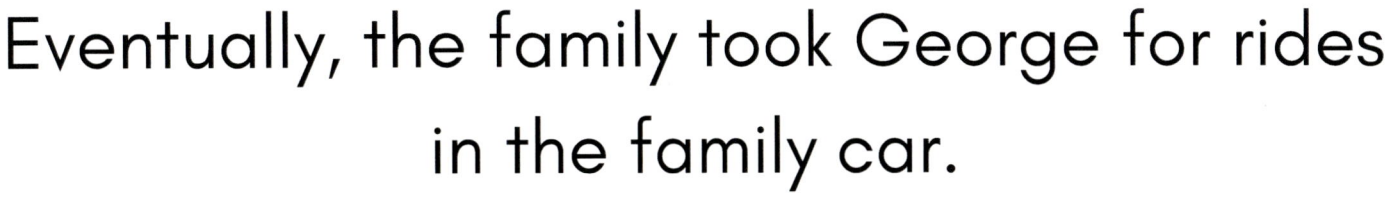

Soon, he began leaning out of the window because he especially loved to hang his head out the window with a big toothless grin on his face.

People in other cars pointed at him with surprised looks on their faces.

On days they went grocery shopping,
they did not take George with them
because the only time they did, he nuzzled his mouth
into the bags looking for his favorite treats.

One bright spring day the family had just returned from grocery shopping and were carrying bags toward the back porch.

Mother noticed that the back door of the house and the gate to George's part of the yard were both wide open.

George was nowhere in sight. "I don't see any of the rest of the animals either. Where are they?"

Everyone ran here and there around the whole yard trying to find George and all the smaller pets.
The yard was empty.

Michael went into the house to look around.
The very last room he entered was his own bedroom.
What he saw there astounded him.

He backed out of his room very quietly and went outside.

"Come see what's in my bedroom."

Everyone followed Michael into the house and looked in the doorway.

After looking at the animals, Father exclaimed, "Well, now we know that George is loved and accepted by all of us. He really is a full-fledged member of our family."

Margaret Sansom - aka Ms. Sam - is a happily retired former teacher of at-risk high school students. Among her adventures since retirement, she has traveled extensively, taken numerous workshops in a wide variety of areas, and started writing children's picture books.

Acknowledgments

I would like to thank all the people who have made my life such a joyful and adventurous journey.
You know who you are.

Ingram Content Group UK Ltd.
Milton Keynes UK
UKRC032130160423
420241UK00001B/6